The Pony-Mad Princess

Princess Ellie's Christmas

Ellie jumped into bed, but found it difficult to go to sleep. She always did on Christmas Eve. Usually that was because she was excited, but this year was different. This year she was worrying too. Her plan was so important. What would she do if it didn't work?

Look out for more sparkly adventures of
The Pony-Mad Princess!

The Pony-Mad Princess

Princess Ellie's Christmas

Diana Kimpton

Illustrated by Lizzie Finlay

USBORNE

In memory of my mum,
who always made Christmas special – LF

First published in 2005 by Usborne Publishing Ltd., Usborne House,
83-85 Saffron Hill, London EC1N 8RT, England. www.usborne.com

Based on an original concept by Anne Finnis.

Cover photograph supplied by Horsepix, Sally and David Waters.

The name Usborne and the devices ♀ ⊕ are
Trade Marks of Usborne Publishing Ltd.

A CIP catalogue record for this book is available from the British Library.

JFMAMJJAS ND/05
ISBN 0 7460 6833 6

Printed in Great Britain.

Chapter 1

"Ouch," said Princess Ellie, as she stabbed herself with the needle. She sucked her sore finger and stared pleadingly at her governess. "Please can I stop sewing now? I want to go to the stables."

"You always do," replied Miss Stringle. "But your ponies will have to wait. You need to finish your mother's present.

The Pony-Mad Princess

It's Christmas Eve tomorrow."

Ellie didn't need reminding. She'd been
looking forward to Christmas for weeks. She
felt as if she'd been sewing for almost as
long. But it was better than lessons,
especially as she could do it in the ruby
sitting room instead of the classroom.

She leaned back in the red velvet
armchair and looked at her
work. The cross-stitched
crown looked lopsided.
"Are you sure Mum
wants an
embroidered
handkerchief?"
she asked.
"I could have
ordered her

something much nicer from the catalogue."
She knew there was no point in suggesting
she bought something in a shop. Princesses
don't go shopping, even at Christmas.

"I've told you before!" declared Miss
Stringle. "The Queen can buy anything she
wants whenever she wants it. So buying her
a present isn't special. It's much better to
make her one."

"I always used to make my mother's
presents when I was a girl," said Great Aunt
Edwina, who was sitting nearby on a red
velvet settee. "Christmas has always been
my favourite time of the year."

"It's mine too," said Ellie, as she started
to sew again. "I want this to be the best
Christmas ever. That's why I want it to
snow."

The Pony-Mad Princess

"It would be wonderful if it did," said the old lady, clapping her hands together in delight. "There has never been a white Christmas at the palace for as long as I can remember."

"Of course there hasn't," said Miss Stringle. "Please remember your geography lessons, Princess Aurelia. We never have snow here."

"We might this year," argued Ellie. "Kate's gran told me to make a wish when I stirred her Christmas pudding mixture. So I wished for snow on Christmas Day – just like there is on all the cards."

Miss Stringle shook her head and sighed. "I'm afraid no amount of wishing will make it snow. No matter what the palace cook believes, there is nothing in a Christmas pudding that can change the weather."

Ellie didn't want to believe her. Surely a wish could work sometimes. She glanced hopefully out of the window. But the sky was clear and blue. There were no clouds in sight.

Great Aunt Edwina didn't seem to notice Ellie's disappointment. She was busy remembering past Christmases. "We always had beautiful decorations when I was a girl."

"We still do," said Ellie, pointing proudly at the Christmas tree in the corner. It was her own special tree and she had decorated it herself. Its branches dripped with silver icicles, golden horseshoes and tiny glass ponies. Sparkly gold tinsel twisted in between them, glinting in the sunlight from the window.

The old lady glanced at the tree. Then she went back to her memories. "We always had wonderful presents when I was a girl."

"That hasn't changed either," said Ellie. "There are heaps of presents under the tree in the ballroom." She sewed the last stitch on the handkerchief and handed it to Miss Stringle. "I've finished now. *Please* say I can go?"

But to Ellie's dismay, her governess produced another handkerchief. "I thought you could do one for Kate as well. It could have a horseshoe instead of a crown."

Ellie stared at her in horror. "Kate's my best friend so I want to give her something she'll be really, really pleased with. And that isn't a hankie – she only uses paper tissues." Just then, she spotted the postman's van through the window and added, "Anyway, I've already ordered her the perfect present. That must be it arriving now."

She raced out of the room and reached the front door at the same time as the postman. Higginbottom, the butler, took the bulging sack from him and tipped the contents onto a table. There were masses of cards, several boring-looking brown envelopes and two parcels.

"Which one's mine?" squealed Ellie, hopping up and down with excitement.

"Neither of them," said Higginbottom. "They're both for His Majesty."

"You must be wrong," cried Ellie. "Kate's present is supposed to come today." She picked up the sack and turned it inside out. But there was no sign of the missing parcel. "What am I going to do?" she groaned.

"Don't panic!" said Higginbottom. "There's another delivery tomorrow morning. That's the last one before Christmas."

His words made Ellie feel slightly better. Tomorrow was Christmas Eve, so if the parcel arrived then she would be able to give Kate the perfect present. But if it didn't come, she'd have nothing to give her at all.

Chapter 2

Ellie burst out laughing when she arrived at the stables and found Meg, the palace groom, wearing a pair of red felt antlers. "I'm just getting in the Christmas mood," Meg explained.

"Look at me!" cried Kate, as she came out of Angel's stable. "Meg's got us some too." The antlers sticking out of her long,

straight hair waggled about as she walked.

"Here are yours," said Meg, holding out an identical pair attached to a hairband.

"Thanks," said Ellie. "They're great." She took off her everyday crown and put on the antlers. Then she tried to balance the crown back in its usual place. But it wouldn't fit. The antlers took up so much space that

there wasn't room for the crown as well.
"Bother," said Ellie.

"Could you leave your crown off just this
once?" said Meg.

Ellie shook her head. "I'll get into trouble
if I'm caught. I'm only allowed to take it off
when I put on my riding hat or my tiara."
Wearing a crown all the time was one of
the annoying parts of being a princess.
The best part was having five
ponies of her own.

"I've got an idea," laughed
Kate. She ran over and took
the crown. Then she stuffed
it on Ellie's head with
one antler poking
through the middle
of it.

The Pony-Mad Princess

Ellie ran into the tack room and stared at herself in the mirror. "That looks really silly," she giggled, as she pulled off the crown. Reluctantly, she took off the antlers and put them on the table. Then she put on her riding hat and said, "Let's go for a ride."

"Can I take Rainbow?" asked Kate. Although Angel was Kate's pony, she was only a foal and much too young to be ridden.

"Of course you can," said Ellie. She knew immediately which pony she wanted to ride. Shadow the Shetland was too small for her and she'd ridden Moonbeam yesterday. Starlight was Angel's mum and needed to stay at home with her foal. So it was obviously Sundance's turn.

16

Princess Ellie's Christmas

The chestnut pony seemed as pleased to be going out as Ellie was. He whickered a welcome as she went into the stable. Then he lowered his head to make it easy for her to put on his bridle, opening his mouth to let her gently slide the bit between his teeth.

As soon as he was ready, Ellie led him outside, tightened his girth and swung herself onto his saddle. She waited until Kate was settled on Rainbow. Then they rode together out of the yard and up a lane that took them deep into the palace grounds.

"I wonder if the ponies know it's nearly Christmas?" said Ellie, as she turned Sundance through an open gate into the deer park. The chestnut pony tossed his head and started to trot as soon as he felt the grass beneath his feet.

"They're very excited," cried Kate, as she struggled to keep Rainbow under control. The grey pony was pulling on the reins, trying to go faster.

"They've got too much energy," laughed Ellie. "Let's use some of it up." She urged Sundance into a canter and then into a gallop. Faster and faster they went until Ellie felt she was almost flying. The wind whistled through her hair as she leaned forward over his neck.

Sundance raced across the deer park with Rainbow close behind. As they neared the wood on the other side, Ellie felt the chestnut pony start to tire. She slowed him to a walk and turned in among the trees onto a path that sloped gently uphill. It was just wide enough for her and Kate to ride side by side.

Rainbow and Sundance didn't try to trot
now. They were happy to walk slowly
through the dappled sunlight that filtered

through the branches. Their hooves scrunched on the soft ground and their ears flicked back and forth as they listened to the sounds of the wood.

Ellie leaned forward and patted Sundance's neck. "They're both calmer now," she said. "But *I'm* still as excited as I was before."

"So am I," agreed Kate. "I can hardly wait until tomorrow. Mum and Dad should be here by ten. I'm not going to bed until they've arrived." Kate didn't see her parents very often because they worked abroad. While they travelled round the world, she stayed with her gran and grandad at the palace so she could go to school.

"Have you told them you're going to be on TV?" asked Ellie.

"Of course I have," said Kate. "They were really surprised. They could hardly believe your parents want everyone in the palace to be in their programme."

"They always do," replied Ellie. The Christmas broadcast was a royal tradition. Every year, on Christmas morning, the King gave a speech to all the people in the kingdom. He liked to wish them Happy Christmas and give them a brief look at the royal celebrations.

Kate ducked to avoid a low branch. "I've never been on TV before. I hope I don't do anything wrong."

"You'll be fine," said Ellie. "Anyway, there's a rehearsal tomorrow morning so you'll have a chance to practise."

She shortened her reins and pushed

21

Sundance into a trot. "Come on. Let's be Christmassy and sing carols." She launched into *Away in a Manger*. Kate joined in and soon they were both singing at the tops of their voices.

As they rode out of the trees onto the open hillside, Ellie looked down at the palace below. There was still no sign of the snow she'd wished for. Perhaps that would come tomorrow, like Kate's present.

Chapter 3

To Ellie's disappointment, Christmas Eve
dawned bright and sunny without a hint of
snow. She was drinking her breakfast orange
juice from a crystal glass when Higginbottom
came into the dining room. He bowed politely
to the King and Queen and announced, "The
TV crew has arrived, Your Majesties. They're
just unloading their equipment."

The Pony-Mad Princess

"I must talk to the director," said the King. He gulped the last of his coffee and strode out of the room. Ellie followed him. She loved watching TV crews at work and knew it would be more fun than eating her toast.

The hall was busy with men carrying cameras, lights and large rolls of cable. In the middle of them stood a woman wearing black trousers and a purple silk shirt embroidered with scarlet dragons.

Her hair was even curlier than Ellie's, but much shorter. It was dyed purple to match her top.

The woman gave the faintest hint of a curtsey and announced, "I'm Gloria Doria, your new director."

"What's happened to the old one?" asked the King, suspiciously.

"He's ill in bed," replied Gloria. "So you've got me instead."

"I hope you know what you're doing," said the King, as he strode towards the ballroom. "This Christmas broadcast is very important to the Queen and me. We want it to be perfect."

Gloria scurried after him. "You needn't worry. I'm one of the top directors in the country. I do all the Albert Blonde films."

The Pony-Mad Princess

"Wow!" said Ellie. She loved watching Albert Blonde, secret agent, save the world from disaster. The special effects in those films were spectacular.

So was the Christmas tree in the ballroom. It was much taller than Ellie's own tree in the ruby sitting room. The footmen had needed to stand on special stepladders to decorate it, and the glittering star on the top touched the ceiling. The tree was laden with gold and silver ornaments encrusted with real jewels, so the multicoloured, twinkling lights were reflected in a thousand diamonds. Piles of exciting-looking presents lay around the base of the tree, waiting to be opened on Christmas morning.

"That's pretty impressive," said Gloria Doria. "Does it do anything?"

The King looked surprised. "It's a tree," he said. "What would you expect it to do?"

"Explode, perhaps," suggested the director.

Ellie put her hand over her mouth to stop herself giggling. Gloria seemed to be having trouble leaving the world of Albert Blonde behind.

The King obviously thought the same. He raised his eyebrows and stared

27

disapprovingly at Gloria. "Royal trees do not explode. They do not revolve and they do not bounce up and down and play carols. Is that understood?"

"Certainly, Your Majesty," replied the director. She looked serious, but the corners of her mouth twitched as if she was trying to hold back a smile.

The King returned his eyebrows to their usual position and continued. "This is the perfect place for me to give my speech. It's traditional for everyone in the palace to gather by this tree on Christmas morning."

"The whole royal family?" asked Gloria.

"And the staff. We give presents to everyone." He glanced at his watch. "They'll all be here in a minute for the rehearsal."

As he spoke, a group of maids walked

nervously into the ballroom. They looked flushed and excited at the thought of being on TV. Ellie was pleased to see Kate arrive next. Her gran was with her. The flour on her apron suggested she had been baking right up to the last minute.

While the TV crew set up the cameras, Gloria organized everyone into a group around the tree. Great Aunt Edwina had a chair because she was old and the King and Queen had their thrones because they were royal. Gloria made Ellie and Kate sit on the floor at the front. "The viewers love to see children at Christmas," she explained.

When everyone was ready, Gloria clapped her hands and shouted, "Action!" Immediately everyone went quiet except the King. He stood up and started his speech.

Ellie quite enjoyed listening to it the first time, but Gloria wasn't satisfied. She made him say it over and over again while she adjusted camera angles and microphones to make it all look perfect on TV.

Finally, she stepped back and sighed. "I'm afraid it's still not right, Your Majesty." She hesitated for a moment. Then she added, "It's just not interesting enough."

"I've spent hours writing that speech," complained the King. "I'm sure the usual director would have liked it."

Gloria smiled apologetically. "It's not the words that are the problem, Your Majesty. It's the pictures. We need some action – something for the viewers to watch."

The King looked at her suspiciously. "I hope you don't want me to do anything silly."

Princess Ellie's Christmas

"Of course not," replied Gloria. "What we need is something Christmassy."

"I've baked some mince pies," suggested Kate's gran. "We could eat those."

"I'm sure the viewers don't want to see us munching," replied the Queen.

"They'd be more interested in the presents," said Ellie.

"That's a brilliant idea," cried Gloria. She grabbed a parcel wrapped in purple paper and read out the label. "To my very best friend, Ellie. With love from Kate."

Kate blushed. "That's mine," she admitted. Then she turned to Ellie and whispered, "You weren't supposed to see it until tomorrow."

Gloria helped Kate to her feet and handed her the parcel. "Now you stand here and give your present to Ellie."

The Pony-Mad Princess

"You mean Princess Aurelia," corrected Miss Stringle from the back of the crowd.

Gloria sighed and shrugged her shoulders. "Okay, Princess Aurelia it is." She turned to Ellie and added, "Come on, love. Up you get."

Ellie heard a sharp intake of breath from the direction of Miss Stringle. Her governess obviously did not approve of princesses being called *love*. But Ellie did. The more she saw of Gloria Doria, the more she liked her.

The director moved the girls around to find the best position for the camera. "Remember, this is just a rehearsal," she said. "You can't open the parcel until we do it for real tomorrow." Then she called "action" again.

Princess Ellie's Christmas

"Happy Christmas!" cried Kate, as she thrust the present into Ellie's hands.

Although they were only pretending, Ellie felt a thrill of excitement. It was such a beautiful parcel that she couldn't resist feeling it. Whatever was inside was very soft.

"That's brilliant," said Gloria. She pointed at Ellie and added, "Now you give your present to Kate."

Ellie stared at the director in horror and then looked back at Kate. How could she tell her best friend that she didn't have a present for her yet?

Chapter 4

There was a long pause while Ellie
wondered desperately what to do. Then
she had an idea. "It isn't here," she
announced. "I haven't wrapped it up yet."
She didn't explain that she hadn't got
anything to wrap.

Luckily, Gloria Doria didn't mind. "We
don't really need to practise that bit."

The Pony-Mad Princess

Kate's gran looked anxiously at her watch. "I need to get back to my baking."

The Queen nodded. "I think we've rehearsed enough. All the staff have a great deal to do today."

As the crowd of people broke up, Ellie spotted the postman's van through the window. "Wait for me here," she told Kate. She slipped quietly out of the room and raced to the hall.

The sack of post was sitting on the table, waiting for Higginbottom to sort it. But there was no sign of the butler. Ellie was too impatient to wait for him. So she tipped up the bag herself and spilled out its contents. Envelopes shot in all directions. Some of them slid across the shiny table and fell onto the floor.

Princess Ellie's Christmas

She didn't bother to pick them up. She wasn't looking for letters or cards. She was only interested in parcels and she hadn't seen any yet. Ellie shook the sack again. There was something in there, but it wouldn't come out.

She peered inside, but it was too dark to see. So she reached into the sack, pushing her hand right to the bottom. Her fingers felt a single parcel. She pulled it free, hoping desperately that it was the one she was waiting for. If it wasn't, she knew she would cry.

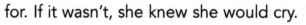

To her relief, the parcel had "Princess Aurelia" written on it in large letters. Next to

The Pony-Mad Princess

the address was a
label announcing
that it came from
Pony Tails magazine.

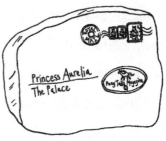

That's where she'd
ordered Kate's present from. At long last,
this was the parcel she'd been expecting.

There wasn't time to open it now
because Kate was waiting for her in the
ballroom. If Ellie took too long, she might
come looking for her and see the parcel.
Then it wouldn't be a surprise.

Ellie knew she needed to hide it until
later. So she ran into the ruby sitting room
and slid the parcel under the settee. She
was sure no one would see it there.

She ran back to the ballroom feeling
much calmer. She had the perfect present

for her best friend. Now she just needed some snow to make it the best Christmas ever.

Kate was still standing beside the tree. The King and Queen and the palace servants had all gone away. The only people left behind were the TV crew, busy putting the finishing touches to their arrangements for the Christmas broadcast.

The chief cameraman walked up to Gloria Doria with a gloomy expression on his face. "I don't like the way it finishes," he moaned. "It just fizzles out."

"I know," agreed Gloria. "It needs something really special to happen at the end."

"How about making the tree explode?" suggested the cameraman. "The special effects team could rig it with some fantastic fireworks."

Ellie couldn't resist interrupting. "I don't

think Dad would like that," she giggled.

"Neither do I," laughed Gloria. "Anyway, fireworks wouldn't look right. We need something Christmassy like robins or crackers or…"

"…Father Christmas?" suggested Ellie.

"That might work," said Gloria, thoughtfully. "We're sure to have a costume in the wardrobe department. I wonder if your butler would dress up in it."

Ellie shook her head. "I don't think so. He only likes wearing his black evening suit."

"I'm sure my grandad would do it," cried Kate. "He played Father Christmas at the school fair and really enjoyed it."

"Brilliant," said Gloria. "But he can't just walk in through the door. That's not exciting enough." She went over to the fireplace and looked up the chimney. "Do you think your grandad could come down *that*?"

Kate stood beside her and peered up into the darkness. "I'm not sure," she said. "It looks very narrow and Gran would be upset if he got stuck."

"I don't expect he'd be very pleased either," said Ellie. "Anyway, it doesn't matter if he fits or not. He can't come down the chimney. It will be too hot. The footmen always light the fire on Christmas morning."

"He could swing in on a rope," suggested the cameraman.

"Or we could strap him to a wire and make it look as if he was flying," added Gloria. "The special effects team are very good at making people fly."

"It's the reindeer that are supposed to fly, not him," said Kate.

Gloria clapped her hands with delight. "That's the answer," she declared. "The highlight of the show will be Father Christmas arriving in the ballroom in a sleigh pulled by reindeer."

"Sleighs are huge," moaned the cameraman. "You'd never get one in here unless those French windows open really wide."

"They do," said Kate. "We rode the ponies through them at the Jubilee party."

"That's settled then," said Gloria.

"No, it's not," said the cameraman, who seemed to enjoy being gloomy. "You won't get hold of a sleigh or reindeer at this time on Christmas Eve. They're all booked up months in advance."

"Oh, dear," said Gloria. "If only there was something else Father Christmas could travel in."

Ellie squealed with excitement. "I know just the thing," she said. But would Gloria Doria agree with her?

Chapter 5

"You need Shadow, my Shetland pony," explained Ellie. "He pulls a carriage that would be perfect for Father Christmas." She grabbed Gloria by the hand and pulled her towards the door. "Come on. I'll show you."

"You'll love him," added Kate, tugging on the director's other hand.

"Okay, okay," laughed Gloria. "Let's go.

Princess Ellie's Christmas

This could be just what we need."

When they arrived at the stables, they found Great Aunt Edwina leaning over Shadow's door. "I've come to see my favourite pony," she explained.

"So have we," said Ellie. She fetched Shadow's headcollar and led the black Shetland pony out into the yard.

"Isn't he sweet!" cooed Gloria Doria.

"Just look at that gorgeous mane and those teeny, tiny hooves."

"You'll love his carriage too," said Ellie.

But Gloria looked disappointed when Meg pulled it out of the barn. "It's very dull. I thought royal carriages were always gold or silver."

"You're thinking of Cinderella's coach," said Kate.

Princess Ellie's Christmas

"That would be perfect," laughed Gloria. "But I don't have a magic wand and a pumpkin to conjure one up. So I'll have to ask the special effects team to brighten up your carriage instead."

"We can do that," cried Ellie, her eyes shining with excitement. "I decorated my tree all by myself. I'm great with tinsel and stuff."

"So am I," declared Kate. "By the time we've finished, it will be perfect for Father Christmas."

"So that's what you're up to," said Great Aunt Edwina, as she gave Shadow a peppermint. He crunched it happily and nuzzled her pocket in search of another one. "I hope your Father Christmas is good at driving ponies."

Kate's mouth dropped open with dismay. "Oh, no!" she groaned. "Grandad has never driven a carriage before."

Ellie sighed. "It was a good idea while it lasted." Then she remembered how much her great aunt enjoyed driving Shadow. "I don't suppose you'd like to be Mother Christmas?" she asked.

"Of course not," declared the old lady. "But I'll happily drive the carriage for Kate's grandfather. Provided I don't have to dress up as an elf."

"I'm sure we can find you something dignified to wear," smiled Gloria. "We've brought loads of costumes with us, just in case." She held her hands in front of her face, pretending they were a camera, and peered through them at Shadow. "It's going to look wonderful when this little fellow trots into the ballroom."

Ellie smiled wistfully. "It'll look even better if my wish comes true and it snows."

"Whatever the weather, let's keep our plan a secret," suggested Gloria. "We want this to be a complete surprise." Then she whisked Great Aunt Edwina away to choose her outfit.

The girls set to work immediately on the carriage. They polished all the woodwork and brushed the dust off the red velvet cushions. Then they fetched saddle soap and metal polish from the tack room and cleaned Shadow's harness until it gleamed.

All that work made them hungry, so they were delighted when a footman arrived with a silver tray piled with food. "The Queen thought you might like your lunch at the

stables as a special Christmas treat,"
he explained.

As they sat in the tack room munching
mince pies and drinking hot chocolate,
Ellie wondered
whether she
should try
to slip away
to wrap
Kate's present.
But there was still so
much to do to the carriage that she didn't
want to waste any time. She was sure the
parcel would be safe in its hiding place. She
could leave it there until the evening and
wrap it after supper.

Just as they finished eating, the chief
cameraman arrived with a large box. It was

Princess Ellie's Christmas

packed with Christmas decorations from Gloria. There were garlands of silver tinsel, silver bells that tinkled as they moved and hundreds of silver star stickers.

Ellie and Kate carefully peeled off the stars one by one and stuck them on the sides of the carriage.

They wound tinsel round and round the long shafts until they couldn't see the wood at all. Then they wound some more round the straps on Shadow's harness. As they worked, they became more and more excited.

"Mum and Dad must be on their way by now," squealed Kate. "I'm so looking forward to seeing them. I'm not going to hang my stocking up until they're here."

"It's a pity Father Christmas doesn't visit the ponies," said Ellie, as she tied bells to the spokes of the wheels. "They miss out on all the fun."

"Perhaps he'd come if we hung stockings up for them," said Kate.

"I've never been allowed to do that," replied Ellie. "I've asked before but George wouldn't let me." George was the old groom who had looked after the ponies before Meg came. He had strict rules and didn't let Ellie help at the stables.

"I'm glad he's not here any more," said Kate, as she reached into the box and pulled out some more tinkling bells.

"So am I," agreed Ellie. Then she smiled mischievously and added, "He can't stop us this year."

"You're right," laughed Kate. "But where can we find six stockings?"

"No problem!" grinned Ellie. "Mum and Dad buy me a new Christmas stocking every year and I always keep the old ones. We can hang up one for each of the ponies and see what happens."

"That sounds fun," said Meg, who had come over to admire their work. "But don't be too disappointed if they're still empty in the morning."

They finished their decorating just in time for tea. The carriage looked magnificent. "It's much better than anything you could get from a pumpkin," said Kate.

"I'll meet you in the yard at seven with the stockings," said Ellie, as they walked back to the palace. That would leave her plenty of time to fetch the hidden parcel and wrap it up.

As soon as she'd finished her meal, Ellie slipped into the ruby sitting room. She kneeled down in front of the settee and reached underneath it. But her searching fingers only found empty air. Kate's present had completely disappeared.

Chapter 6

Ellie slumped onto the sitting room floor, feeling miserable and confused. Where could the parcel have gone? What would she do if she couldn't find it?

"Is this what you're looking for?" asked a voice from behind her.

She turned round and saw Miss Stringle holding the missing package. Ellie was so pleased that she nearly kissed her. But she stopped herself just in time and asked, "Where did you find it?"

Miss Stringle smiled. "I was playing chess with your great aunt when the maids moved the settee to clean the carpet. I picked it up as soon as I saw it was addressed to you." She shook the parcel gently. "Is it something important?"

"It's Kate's present," replied Ellie, as she ripped off the paper. "It's a T-shirt with a heart-shaped picture of Angel and the words 'I love Angel' written on it in bright red letters."

The T-shirt was neatly folded in a plastic bag. She pulled it out and held it up with the decorated side facing her governess. "Do you like it? I took the photo myself."

Princess Ellie's Christmas

Miss Stringle looked puzzled. "But I thought Angel was a foal?"

Ellie turned the T-shirt round and stared at it in dismay. The words were perfect but the heart-shaped picture wasn't. Instead of Kate's pretty skewbald foal, it showed a huge, fat carthorse with one blue eye and one brown eye. He was much bigger than Angel and nowhere near as pretty.

"It's the wrong photo," she wailed. "What am I going to do?"

"You'll have to send it back," said Miss Stringle. "It's their mistake, so they're sure to replace it with one that's correct."

The Pony-Mad Princess

"But there isn't time," groaned Ellie, forcing back the tears that pricked at her eyes. "I won't have anything to give Kate in the morning."

"Yes, you will," declared Miss Stringle. She handed Ellie a plain, white handkerchief. "I'm sure you can embroider a horseshoe this evening if you sew fast enough."

Ellie took it without any enthusiasm. She still didn't want to give Kate a hankie with a wonky horseshoe. But she didn't have a choice. It would be even worse to give nothing at all to her best friend.

She trudged up the spiral staircase to her bedroom and tipped the contents of her sewing box onto her quilt. The brightly coloured embroidery threads looked much more cheerful than she felt. It was hard to choose the best one for Kate, but Ellie finally picked a shiny thread with real gold twisted into it. Maybe that would make the hankie look special.

She soon wished she had made a different choice. The gold thread was stiffer than the ordinary ones and much harder to sew with. Each stitch took ages. She had only done three by the time her pink alarm clock told her it was nearly seven. It was time to meet Kate.

Ellie dumped the sewing on her bed. She'd have to finish it later. Then she pulled out her box of keepsakes from under her bed and grabbed six old Christmas stockings.

As she ran downstairs with them, the excitement of Christmas Eve pushed away her disappointment about the present. The palace twinkled with decorations. Hundreds of Christmas cards adorned the walls and, somewhere in the distance, the maids were singing carols.

Her excitement evaporated as soon as she saw Kate. Her friend was standing beside Angel's stable with her shoulders slumped miserably. Her face was streaked with tears and her eyes were red from crying.

"What's wrong?" asked Ellie.

"It's Mum and Dad," sobbed Kate. "Their car broke down on the way to the airport. They've missed the last plane home. There's no way they can be here for Christmas."

Ellie put her arm round her friend's

shoulders and gave her a hug. She felt like crying too. She knew how much Kate had been looking forward to seeing her parents. It just wasn't fair.

"They'll be here the day after tomorrow," sighed Kate. "Gran says we can have another Christmas dinner then. But it won't be the same. We'll only be pretending."

"I'm really sorry," said Ellie, trying to think of a way to cheer her friend up. Then she remembered the stockings and waved them in Kate's face. "Let's hang these up. It'll get us back in the Christmas mood."

Kate smiled weakly and chose a stocking decorated with stars. "This one can be for

Angel." She hung it beside her stable, making sure it was out of the foal's reach. Ellie hung another stocking beside it for Starlight.

"They look really Christmassy," said Kate. "Let's hang up the others."

Moonlight, Sundance and Rainbow poked their heads out of their stables to see what was happening. Shadow didn't. He was so small that he couldn't put his head over his door. So he banged it with his hooves to attract Ellie's attention.

She waved the stocking over the door. "You don't want this," she explained. "It's empty. But it might not be in the morning if Father Christmas comes."

"I don't expect he will," groaned Kate. "Everything's going wrong this year."

Princess Ellie's Christmas

Ellie nodded in agreement. She so wanted this to be the best Christmas ever, but it was starting to look as if it would be the worst one. Then suddenly she thought of a plan – one that could solve everything. But she couldn't do it on her own.

Chapter 7

Ellie knew there was no time to waste. If her plan was going to work, she had to ask for help as soon as possible. "I've got to get back," she told Kate. "I've still got your present to wrap." She didn't mention that she hadn't made it yet.

She left her friend talking to Angel and ran back to the palace. There was no sign of her parents in the King's office, the Queen's study or the ruby sitting room. She finally found them in the parlour, eating toasted marshmallows while they watched TV.

The King held out the dish. "Have one, Aurelia. They're delicious."

The Pony-Mad Princess

The sight of the sweets made Ellie's mouth water. She longed to take one, but she knew she shouldn't. It was going to be hard to persuade her parents to help. It would be even harder if she was mumbling through a mouthful of marshmallow. So she resisted the temptation and announced, "I've got a brilliant idea."

"Oh dear," said the Queen, with a worried look on her face. Some of Ellie's previous ideas had turned out not to be as brilliant as she'd first thought.

"I hope it's not going to cause trouble," said the King. "We don't want anything to spoil Christmas."

"This won't," cried Ellie. "I promise." She explained her plan as quickly as she could.

Princess Ellie's Christmas

The King looked doubtful. "It's a lovely idea. I'm just not sure if it will work."

"I don't think there's enough time," added the Queen, looking at her watch.

"Please try," begged Ellie. "Please, please, *please.*"

To her relief, they finally agreed. The King made several phone calls. Then he summoned Higginbottom and told the butler about the important task they wanted him to do.

Once Ellie knew her plan was under way, she went back to her bedroom and her sewing. She was still working on the hankie when the Queen came to kiss her goodnight.

"Don't stay up too long," she said, as she helped Ellie hang her stocking on the end of her pink, four-poster bed. "Father Christmas never comes while you're awake."

The Pony-Mad Princess

Ellie knew that was true. But Kate's present was more important, so she kept sewing late into the night. When she finished the last stitch, she snipped off the thread and stared at her handiwork. The horseshoe looked even wonkier than she'd expected, but it was better than no present at all.

She carefully folded the hankie and wrapped it in beautiful, blue paper decorated with golden horseshoes. Then she wrote, "To Kate, my best friend in all the world" on the label in gold ink. It wasn't the perfect present, like she'd hoped, but it still looked pretty.

She crept downstairs and put the tiny

Princess Ellie's Christmas

parcel beside the large one Kate was giving her. The ballroom was empty and quiet. It seemed to be holding its breath, waiting for Christmas to come. The twinkling lights on the huge tree looked more beautiful than ever in the darkness.

Back in her room Ellie jumped into bed, but found it difficult to go to sleep. She always did on Christmas Eve. Usually that was because she was excited, but this year was different. This year she was worrying too. Her plan was so important. What would she do if it didn't work?

She tried counting ponies. She tried counting princesses and she tried counting Kings. But sleep wouldn't come. There were too many thoughts going round in her head.

Eventually she dozed. When she woke,

69

The Pony-Mad Princess

it was still dark. She reached out her foot
and touched her stocking, hoping it would
feel lumpy and exciting. But it didn't. It was
still completely empty. Ellie sighed. So much
had already gone
wrong that she
wouldn't be
surprised if Father
Christmas didn't
come at all.

  The next time
she woke, light
was streaming
through the
curtains. She
looked down
at the end of the
bed and grinned.

Princess Ellie's Christmas

Her stocking was stuffed with exciting packages. One of them was so long that it stuck right out of the top.

She bounced out of bed, feeling thoroughly Christmassy. At last, something had happened the way she wanted. Perhaps her wish had come true too. "Please, please let there be snow," she pleaded as she opened the curtains. But there wasn't. The view from her window looked exactly the same as it always did, and the sky was clear and blue, without a hint of a cloud.

Ellie tried not to feel too disappointed. It wouldn't be too bad if that was the only thing that went wrong today. She would be much more upset if her plan failed.

Chapter 8

Ellie bounced out of bed and threw on her riding clothes. Then she grabbed her stocking and ran through the silent palace to her parents' room. "Happy Christmas," she shouted, as she popped her head round the door. "Is there any news of my plan?"

"Happy Christmas," yawned the King. "We haven't heard anything yet, but I'm sure Higginbottom is doing his best."

"You'll know as soon as he gets back," added the Queen. She sat up in bed, popped her everyday crown on top of her curlers and gave Ellie a hug. "Now let's see what Father Christmas has brought you."

The Pony-Mad Princess

Ellie quivered with excitement as she sat on their bed and started to open her presents. The long parcel contained five pink saddlecloths rolled up together. Each of them had silver ribbon round the edge and the name of one of her ponies sewn on it in silver braid.

Further down the stocking was a new pink and gold cover for her riding hat, the latest book in her favourite series about ponies, and a large chocolate horseshoe.

 She bit off one end and munched it while she opened the last parcel. It was a tin of glittering, silver hoof polish. "Wow!" said Ellie. "That's just what I need for Shadow."

Princess Ellie's Christmas

She stuffed everything else back in her stocking. Then she gave her Mum and Dad a Christmas kiss, picked up the hoof polish and raced down to the stables.

Kate caught up with her just outside the yard. "Look what I've got," she cried, waving a purple headcollar that was the perfect size for Angel. "It was in my stocking with a book on training foals."

"I wonder if the ponies have got anything in theirs," said Ellie. She hardly dared to look.

Kate was bolder. She stepped into the yard and yelled, "He's been, he's been."

Ellie followed her and squealed with delight. All the ponies' stockings were bulging with carrots. Angel had a purple lead rope that matched her new headcollar. Each of Ellie's ponies had a pink and silver browband for their bridles that matched their new saddlecloths.

"That's amazing," said Meg, when she came to see what all the noise was about. "I've never heard of ponies getting presents from Father Christmas before."

The mention of Father Christmas reminded Ellie of the royal broadcast. "Does your grandad like the outfit Gloria found for him?" she asked.

Kate nodded. "He put it on last night to show us. He looked so funny that he really cheered me up." She went quiet for a moment and added wistfully, "I wish Mum and Dad were here to see him. Christmas doesn't feel the same without them."

Princess Ellie's Christmas

"I'm sorry," sighed Ellie.

"You'd both better cheer up and get to work," said Meg, as she led Shadow into the yard. "You haven't got long to get him ready and he's really dirty." The Shetland pony had obviously been lying down during the night. His mane and tail were full of straw and his legs were covered with manure stains.

Ellie and Kate brushed and brushed until he was completely clean. By the time they had finished, his black coat gleamed in the sunshine and his long mane and tail were free of tangles. They put on the harness they had decorated the day before. Then they plaited tinsel into his mane, tied a huge tinsel bow on the top of his tail, and used Ellie's new hoof oil to paint his hooves silver.

The Pony-Mad Princess

Kate stepped back to admire their work. "He looks fantastic. Father Christmas couldn't do better unless he had a real reindeer."

That gave Ellie an idea. She ran to the tack room and fetched the antlers Meg had given her. Very carefully, she tied them to the top of Shadow's bridle, making sure

they wouldn't fall off when he moved. "Now he really is a reindeer," she laughed.

"Gloria Doria will love him," said Kate.

"But my mum and dad won't love us if we're late," added Ellie, glancing at her watch. "We'd better get ourselves ready now."

"I'm looking forward to really giving you your present," said Kate, as they ran back to the side door of the palace.

Ellie gulped. She wasn't looking forward to giving Kate hers.

Chapter 9

Ellie showered quickly and put on her special Christmas dress. She had a new one every year and her parents always chose it for her. This one was pink, like all her other clothes, and made of shimmery satin decorated with golden ruffles. As soon as she had fastened the zip, she popped a sparkly tiara on her head, slipped her feet

into a pair of gold sandals, and ran down
to the ballroom.

It looked even more festive than yesterday.
There was a log fire crackling in the fireplace,
towers of red and gold crackers, and crystal
dishes full of nuts and sweets.

As Ellie went to join the crowd in front of
the tree, she was surprised to see that the
curtains at one end of the room were still
closed.

"It's to make sure Shadow is
a big surprise," whispered
Gloria, who had crammed
a Father Christmas hat on
top of her purple curls.
"We don't want anyone
noticing the French windows
are open until we're ready."

"But how will they see Shadow arrive?" asked Ellie.

"That's your job. When you hear his bells tinkling, I want you and Kate to run over to the window and open the curtains."

Ellie started to walk away. Then she turned back and whispered, "There may be another surprise too."

"Your father's already told me all about that," laughed Gloria. "If your plan works, it will make the broadcast even better."

By now, it was nearly time for the programme to begin. The King was pacing up and down nervously, practising his Christmas message. Almost everyone else was already in the right place.

"Have you seen Great Aunt Edwina?" asked the Queen.

"Err… She's not coming," said Ellie. Her mind raced as she struggled to think of a believable excuse. "She's got a headache."

It wasn't a very convincing lie, but it seemed to satisfy the Queen. "Oh dear," she said. "I do hope she'll be better in time for dinner."

A bell rang. "One minute to broadcast," called Gloria. "Places everyone."

Ellie sat down close to Kate and looked round at the sea of faces. To her disappointment, her great aunt wasn't the only person missing. Higginbottom was nowhere to be seen. He was a vital part of her plan. If he didn't get back soon, she would know for sure that her plan had completely failed.

"Action," called Gloria. They all waved at

the cameras as they'd rehearsed. Then the King stood up and started his speech.

Ellie knew she was supposed to look at him while he was speaking. But her eyes kept straying to the huge double doors that led to the hall. They stayed stubbornly shut. There was still no sign of Higginbottom.

The King stopped talking and sat down. Everyone looked at the girls as Kate thrust her present into Ellie's hands. "Happy Christmas," she said, loudly. Then she added in a whisper, "It's just what you want."

For a brief moment, Ellie wondered if she could put off opening the parcel so she didn't have to give hers to Kate. Then her excitement got the better of her and she tore open the paper.

Princess Ellie's Christmas

Inside was a beautiful fleecy top. It was
soft and fluffy and, best of all, it wasn't pink
like Ellie's other clothes.
It was a gorgeous
pale purple – her
favourite colour.
She put it on
straight away.
It looked strange
over her new
dress, but it
felt wonderful.
"Thank you,"
she said. "It's fantastic."

"Now give her yours," whispered the
Queen. "Everyone's waiting."

Ellie glanced at the doors again. They
were still shut. Dismally, she picked up the

tiny parcel and handed it to Kate. "Happy Christmas," she said. "I'm sorry it's so small."

Kate read the gold writing on the label and smiled. At that moment, a slight movement attracted Ellie's attention. Her heart missed a beat as she realized the double doors were opening. Perhaps there was hope after all. A few seconds later, Higginbottom slipped into the room and gave her a thumbs-up signal.

Kate ripped the paper open and pulled out the small square of white cloth. "It's a hankie," she said in a surprised voice.

"It's...um...to cover your eyes," cried Ellie. "You must keep them closed until I tell you to open them."

She waited until she was sure her friend

wasn't peeking. Then she ran out through the double doors to fetch Kate's real present.

Chapter 10

Out in the hall, Ellie met the two people she most wanted to see. The man was tall, bearded and tanned by the sun. The woman was shorter, with straight brown hair just like Kate's. They both looked rather nervous at being in the palace.

"I'm so pleased you're here," said Ellie. "You're just in time." She took them by the hand and led them to the huge tree in the ballroom. Kate couldn't see them. She was standing with her eyes screwed up tight, holding the hankie over her face.

Ellie carefully positioned the two visitors in front of her. When she was sure they were in the best possible place, she called, "You can look now."

Kate lowered the hankie and opened her eyes. Instantly, her face lit up with delight. "Mum and Dad!" she squealed, trying to hug them both at once. "But you said you couldn't get here. You said you'd missed the last plane."

"We had," said her dad, as he wrapped his arms round her in an enormous hug. "But then Princess Aurelia stepped in to help."

The Pony-Mad Princess

Kate looked at Ellie. "What did you do?"

Ellie grinned. "I talked Mum and Dad into sending the royal jet to fetch them." Before she could say any more, she heard the sound of tinkling bells. Immediately, she grabbed Kate by the hand and dragged her towards the end of the room. "Come on. Let's see what's outside."

Princess Ellie's Christmas

As they pulled the curtains open, Ellie gasped with surprise. Outside the French windows was a winter wonderland. Sunlight twinkled on a thick layer of snow that carpeted the palace garden. Icicles hung from the window frames and dripped from the snow-covered branches of the nearby trees. It looked just like a Christmas card.

The Pony-Mad Princess

To make the picture perfect, Shadow trotted into view. He pulled his carriage proudly, as if he knew he was the star of the show. Ellie and Kate's decorations looked fantastic. The tinsel and silver bells made the carriage sparkle. Shadow's mane and tail sparkled too. His reindeer antlers bobbed gently every time his glittery, silver hooves touched the ground.

Princess Ellie's Christmas

Great Aunt Edwina smiled happily as she held the reins. Her red silk dress and wide-brimmed hat were trimmed with silver to match the carriage. She looked almost as festive as Kate's grandad, who was sitting beside her in his Father Christmas outfit. He was obviously enjoying himself. His blue eyes twinkled behind his fake, white beard.

As Shadow trotted into the ballroom, they both waved and shouted, "Happy Christmas!"

Everyone shouted "Happy Christmas" back. Then they crowded excitedly around the carriage to get a better look at the new arrivals.

The King waved happily at the nearest camera. "Happy Christmas to you all," he declared, as everyone cheered and clapped.

"Cut," called Gloria. "Well done! That was the perfect end to a brilliant broadcast."

"And a wonderful surprise," said the Queen.

Kate put her arms round Ellie and hugged her. "Thanks a million. You've given me the perfect present."

"That's what friends are for," said Ellie. "But there's one thing I don't understand. Where has all that snow come from?"

Gloria winked at her and laughed. "Sometimes wishes need a bit of help from the special effects team."

Ellie took a peppermint from one of the crystal dishes and gave it to Shadow. While he crunched it, she looked at Kate smiling happily as she snuggled close to her parents. She looked at the sparkling carriage

and Father Christmas in his bright red outfit.
But most of all, she looked at the snow.
"This is definitely the best Christmas ever,"
she announced. "Wishes sometimes *do*
come true."

Look out for more sparkly
adventures of

The Pony-Mad Princess

coming soon...

Princess Ellie
Saves the Day